I bet She Called me Sugar plum

I bet She called me Sugar plum

By Joanne V. Gabbin
Illustrated by Margot Bergman
Foreword by Lucille Clifton

 Franklin Street Gallery Productions
Harrisonburg, Virginia

Book Design by Sang Yoon

Library of Congress Cataloging-in-Publication Data

I Bet She Called Me Sugar Plum/by Joanne V. Gabbin;
illustrated by Margot Bergman; foreword by
Lucille Clifton.
ISBN 0-9760716-0-6

Printed by
Franklin Street Gallery Productions
150 Franklin Street
Harrisonburg, VA 22801

http://www.sugarplumgabbin.com

DEDICATION

Dedicated to the memory of my mother,
Jessie Smallwood Veal (1914-1970),
who taught the lesson of the closed hand and the dime.

To the memory of Dione Andrea Vieira Hunt (1974-2003),
whose angelic smile and soft-spoken voice
remain constant in my thoughts.

To the memory of my niece, Jessica Sha Ron Veal (1973-2003),
who delighted in hearing Grandma's stories.

J.V.G.

DEDICATION

In memory of my mother, Margaret Haynes Foster.
She taught me about love and
how to be a mother.
She shared with me the fun of sewing and
making things, dancing, reading, and play.

M.B.

FOREWORD

How important it is that we do something to combat
the imagery surrounding us today. It has not always
been so; the pictures that we see, hear, and feel
around us are not sustaining ones. That is only one
of the reasons that we greet this book with such joy.
We seem to have forgotten how to be sustaining,
nourishing, even kind to and for our children. How
important then that we have this lovely and honest
book! Let our children realize the power of calmness
and of love! Let them be aware of a family feeling
that is bound by more than blood, more than class;
that is kept alive by love.

Lucille Clifton

"Mama, please tell me about Grandma. I want to hear once more

About the little garden that she planted around her door."

Sweetie, in a patch no bigger than a yard,

Your grandma planted cabbage, beans, and
bright red rhubarb.

Well, your grandma always bought our groceries in bushels and fifty-pound sacks.

We would load our long, green car from the very front to the back.

Then she'd call all the neighbors, and each one would bring a bag

And load it up with our groceries until it almost sagged.

I didn't understand why she gave so much away
When we had worked so hard to collect it all that day.

So your grandma placed a dime in the center of my hand,

And told me, "Close your fingers as tightly as you can."

Then she tried to put a quarter into my
balled-up fist.

"You see, Sugar," she said, "nothing can get out,
but nothing can get in."

"Mama, I like to hear that story of how much Grandma shared.

I always will remember just how much my grandma cared."

"Mama, tell me about the game—you know the one,

When she called you every sweet name under
the sun."

Oh! I remember all the lovely names: Dumpling,
Sugar Lump, and Sweet Potato Pie,

But I loved it most when she called me the "apple
of her eye."

"Mama, please tell me did I grow inside of you and swell you like a spinning top?

Did I grow and grow until you looked like you would pop?"

No, Sweetie, not under my heart, but in it you grew until I was ripe for your coming,

And Daddy and I brought you home in a little yellow bunting.

Another mommy first kissed your cheeks and touched your soft brown hair.

Another mommy loved you and left you to our care.

"Mama, please tell me one more thing before I go
     to sleep.

          What did my first mommy call me when she
          stroked my cheek?"

Sweetheart . . . I don't know how she could
pick just one . . .

"Oh! I know, I know Mama, I bet
   she called me Sugar Plum!"

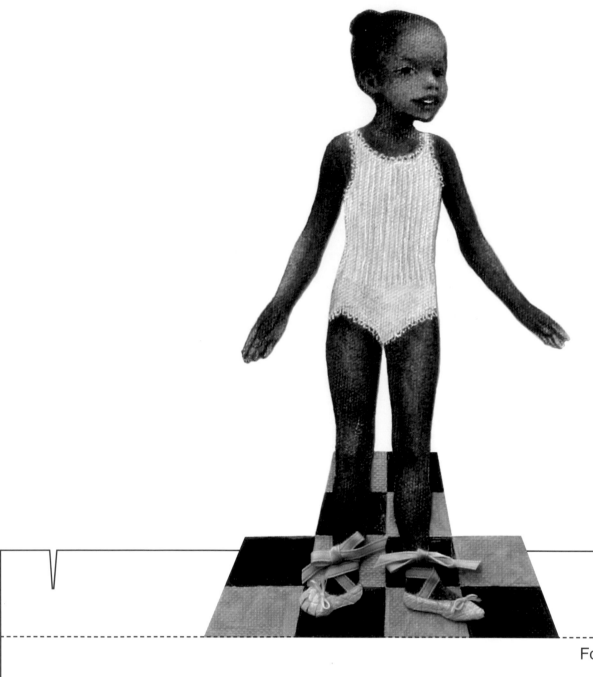

Fold then cut slits

Glue
or tape
to
her
back
↓

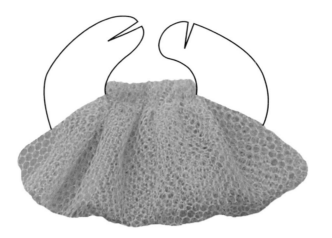

Joanne V. Gabbin, *author*

The joy of creating *I Bet She Called Me Sugar Plum* grows out of my respect and love for parenthood and my desire to see children in loving, protective homes. It is a touching book about the love between a mother and daughter and the safe place that their love creates. In the stories that they share, there are always discoveries: a grandmother's wisdom, a parent's joy, and a child's curiosity about her origins. The child delights in hearing stories about her grandmother over and over again, and these stories often teach lessons about nature, generosity, and kindness. Using a poetic dialogue to bring life to the two characters, I approach questions about pregnancy, adoption, self-awareness, and self-esteem. The little girl who emerges from the pages of this book is confident, inquisitive, reflective, and secure.

My excitement for *I Bet She Called Me Sugar Plum* also comes out of my association with artist Margot Bergman, whose enthusiasm for this project is evident in the exquisite collages that she created. Her collages with textures that range from prickly burlap to delicate lace to silky satin entice the book's readers to run their fingers over its pages. She lovingly crafts each art piece to suggest the warmth and affection of the mother-daughter relationship. The book is our testament to reflections on our own upbringing, the memories we cherish of our mothers, and the joy we have experienced as parents.

Oil portrait by Margot Bergman

Joanne V. Gabbin, a native of Baltimore, Maryland, is the author of *Sterling A. Brown: Building the Black Aesthetic Tradition*, and the editor of *The Furious Flowering of African American Poetry* and *Furious Flower: African American Poetry from the Black Arts Movement to the Present*. With teaching, poetry, and art as three guiding passions, she gives her energy to directing the Honors Program and the Furious Flower Poetry Center at James Madison University and owning and directing the 150 Franklin Street Gallery in Harrisonburg, Virginia. This is her first children's book.

Margot Bergman, *illustrator*

Joanne Gabbin had not yet written the poem when she approached me about making the illustrations. She described the story to me, and I was really touched by it. We had already shared feelings about our children, and we vibrated together on this theme.

I immediately had an impression of how the illustrations should look! The process should embody playfulness, almost like the diversions I used to create with my child when he was little. I wanted to shift freely between realistic representation and constructions using found objects, beads, and fabrics, in a way that would surprise and tickle the imagination of the viewer. But the pictures also had to show real convincing characters and the love relationship between them.

The poem doesn't use many words, but it shouldn't be rushed through. So the illustrations are full of details to dwell upon and suggest something of the full scope of family life that envelopes the narrative. The ongoing conversation between the mother and the daughter takes place over the span of an afternoon and evening. The stories they share about the grandmother go back to when the mother was a child. These illustrations appear in a round format and are slightly more abstract to distinguish them as somewhat remote in time.

Watercolor self-portrait

Margot Bergman was born into an artistic family and has followed this path from an early age, making art and also teaching art and aesthetics at the university level. She received her M.F.A. from James Madison University. Her portraits in oil and pencil are widely known. She works in many media and for the past ten years has been exploring the form of the "radical art quilt." The contemporary artists that have inspired her include Faith Ringgold, Romare Bearden, and Red Grooms. Her work is distinctly lyrical with feminine values of relationship between people and connection with spirit and nature.